THE INFLATABLES

in AIR TO THE THRONE

DIVE INTO THE DEEP END
with more inflatable adventures!

THE INFLATABLES in AIR TO THE THRONE

By Beth Garrod & Jess Hitchman
Illustrated by Chris Danger

Scholastic Inc.

To our inflata-readers, especially Aanand and Hrithik - you rule the pool! —BG

For my excellent pal Jossy —JH

To my brother from another mother, Christian Arichabala —CD

Chapter One

Once upon a Swim Cap

Everything was perfect at the best place on earth: the Lost and Found pool.

But somebody didn't think so . . .

2

4

5

Look, I made an ice cream sculpture!

MELTED ICE CREAM SOUP

And painted a beautiful mural!

DO NOT SWIM IN A POOL LIKE THIS.

And changed the sign so it says PALACE!

LOST & FOUND
POO LACE

SPELLING NEEDS WORK

Hmm, if I'm going to make the perfect home for my inflata-pals, I need to put my thinking cap on!

But I don't have a thinking cap!

I will find a thinking cap! Good thinking, Flamingo.

Hey, how did I think of that without a thinking cap?

9

A-WHOOSH!!

Bless you.
Are you okay?

Oops, let me try that again. **KAZAM!**

What IS
happening
to you?!

I'm trying to appear in a magical puff
of smoke, but it isn't working. So
anyway, I'm your Airy Frogfather.

AIRY FROGFATHER

NEWT TO THE JOB

TOAD-ALLY TERRIFIC TUTU

MAGIC WAND/STICK THING

12

Chapter Two
A Legend-airy Tale

For years, inflatables have competed to wear that crown and restore the palace to glory. But it will only fit the head of the true air to the throne.

Many have tried and failed. Until . . .

Hey, that's my hat!!! Oh wait, that's me!

Now Flamingo can claim the palace as his own and live happily air-ver after.

JOURNEY TO THE THRONE

SLIDE 9¾

YOUR QUEST STARTS HERE

Uh . . . guys? Slide 9³/₄ was never finished. And that forest looks gnarly!

But our new and improved home is waiting for us. Let's go!

Bye-bye, Lost and Found pool! Bye-bye, Ice Cream Jean's truck! Bye-bye, pool tile that looks like my face! And puddle where my reflection looks great! I'll miss you all!

I'm sure nothing will go wrong on our biggest adventure yet, set by a frog in a rather delightful skirt . . .

Oh, rollicking ribbits! I forgot to tell them about the extremely dangerous baddie who wants to pop them!

EXTREME DANGER WARNING TO THE AIR TO THE THRONE

AIRY FROGFATHER

Name: Sir Spits-A-Lot
Friends call him: His Most Evil Evilington. Or Steve.

‼   ‼

Under **NO** circumstance can you forget to tell the air to the throne about Sir Spits-A-Lot, the inflatable llama who currently lives in the castle and is refusing to budge:

· **Wears a fake crown he swears is real.**

· **Has the palace guarded by an army of inflata-llamas, who are very bitey.**

⭐·Fun fact: When annoyed, llamas can spit up to fifteen feet. ⭐⭐

· Even funner fact: Fifteen feet is almost half the length of a school bus. So always sit near the back if there's a llama driving! ⭐

· **Hobbies include staring into his crystal beach ball, gardening, and being really, really mean.**

· **Hobbies also include filling inflatable intruders with concrete.**

· **Is obsessed with fluffy quokkas, the cutest animal in the world.**

21

Chapter Three
Airway to Heaven

24

25

Guess I've got to do what the Airy Frogfather said. If I want the perfect new home for my pals, I HAVE to be brave.

We can be brave together. Everyone?

INFLATABLES ASSEMBLE!

26

And then the inflatables whooshed off on the wettest, weirdest, and windiest waterslide of their lives.

ZOO

AQUARIUM

LIBRARY

CAFÉ

UNFINISHED END

SPACE

27

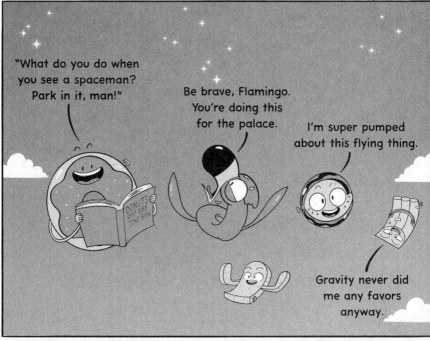

28

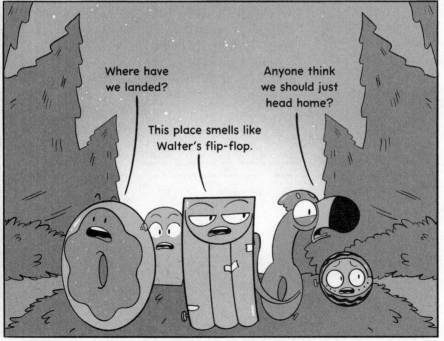

31

34

35

Chapter Four

The Big Bad Waffle

Oh, flap! We'll never get through this giant door.

Um, you could try just pushing it . . .

Oh, pips! We'll never get through this giant door.

I know what might help. A snack! A cookie helps everything.

Hey! That hurt!

I don't think that's a cookie, Donut . . .

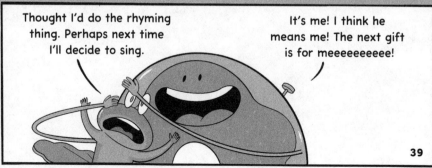

41

42

43

44

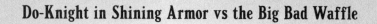

Do-Knight in Shining Armor vs the Big Bad Waffle

ROUND 1
Winner: The Big Bad Waffle!

49

ROUND 3
Winner: Do-Knight in Shining Armor!

50

Crunch! Chew!
Munch . . . Ew!

54

Ecin yrev yllautca saw elppa eht.

IT'S GETTING WORSE!!

Mirror, mirror on the wall. Who's the air-est of them all? Me? Why, thank you.

NO! Focus, Flamingo! Mirror, mirror on the wall. How do we get Watermelon back to nor-mall?

This mirror is no use! We need to think of something else.

We could follow the signs for Happyville? Maybe someone there can help us.

HAPPYVILLE

PERFECT! The happy people will help us. Inflatables, assemble!

Elbmessa, selbatalfni!

HAPPYVILLE

56

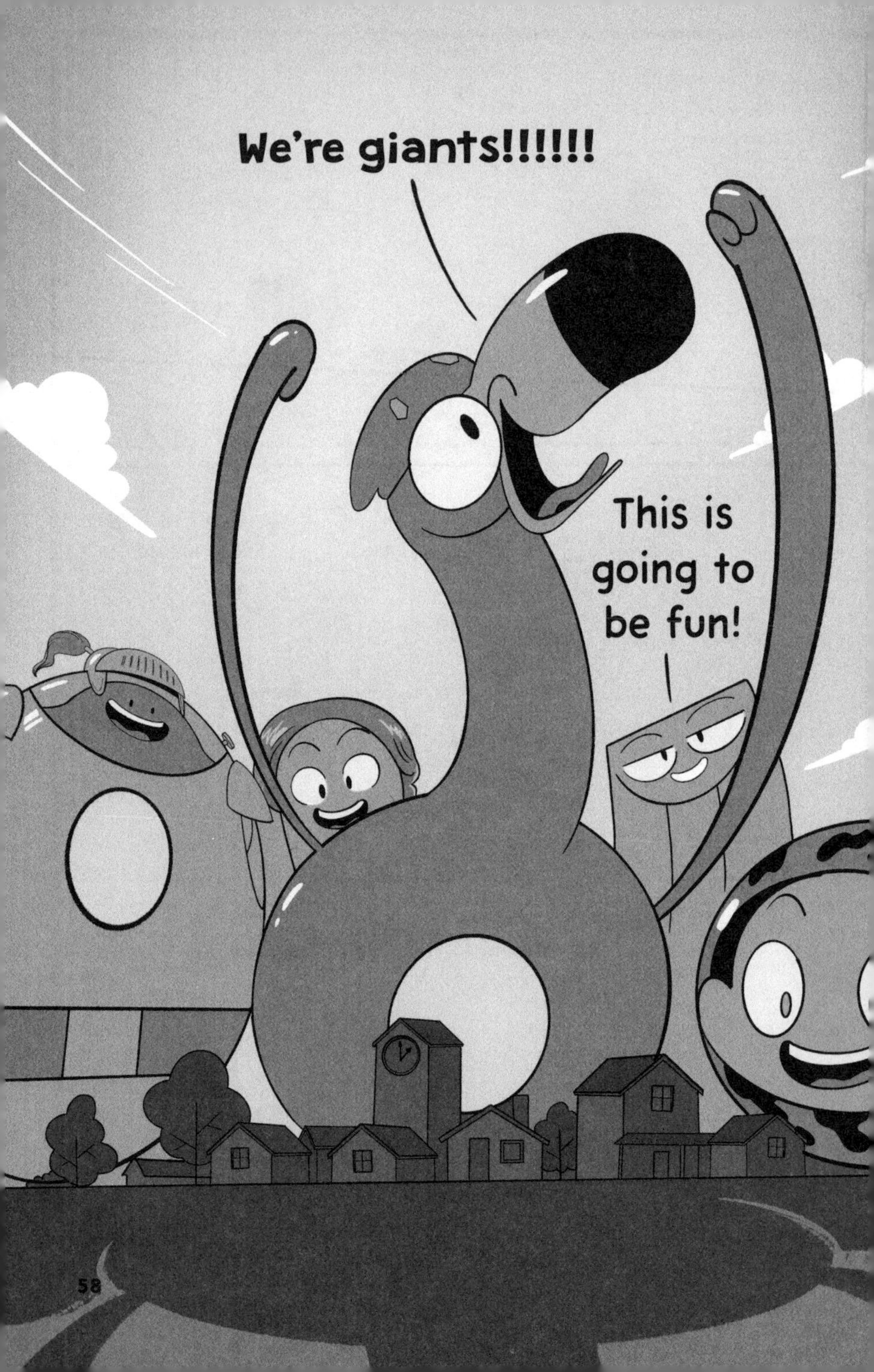
We're giants!!!!!!
This is going to be fun!

60

61

.stod ni doog yllaer kool I, yeH

Hey, I look really good in dots.

Awwww, my cute dots went away!

I un-poisoned you and that's all you have to say?!

Anyhoo, now that Watermelon is normal, we can finally enjoy Happyville. Get that dinner cooking, Star!

KISS THE CHEF

Everyone, hold your breath!

And ruuuuuuun!

Chapter Six
All Fired Up

Hey, warty green thing. I want a word.

SNAP

KAZOOK! Normally I wouldn't answer to that, but . . . well . . . you scare me.

So where's *my* gift?

Another mirror?

A TADPOLE

FROGSPAWN

GETTING HIS FIRST TUTU

LIFE FLASHING BEFORE EYES

I like it. Looking at myself is a great way to spend any day.

Wasn't that MY mirror?

Have some free potion instead. It's actually a very magical gift. I just forgot I had it.

70

"Why did the baker give up baking donuts? *He was fed up with the hole business!*"

"What's the difference between a fish and a piano? You can't tuna fish."

I'll pass.

"Why did the golfer wear two pairs of trousers? In case she got a hole in one."

75

Chapter Seven
Llamageddon

Statues? You mean the inflatables filled with concrete?

YIKES!

All right, Flamingo. You've come this far. You can do this! Get that butt on the throne. And get rid of that meanie Sir Spits-A-Lot!

If only there was a sign. Something to tell me that everything's gonna be okay!

OMG! It's a sign! Look at all those fluffy clouds! Everything's gonna be okay!

Llazy—Will pop you if she can be bothered.

Lleaky—Lets out deadly air . . . regularly.

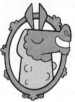

Llumpy—Lleader of the gang.

Lloudmouth—Can pop you with one shriek.

Lleafy—Always got her head in a bush.

Llovely—Definitely not lovely. His dad thought the name might help.

Llaughy—Watch out for his killer giggle.

Llucky—Thinks she's a dog.

Lleo—Thinks she's a lion.

Llucy—Surprisingly reasonable.

Cllive—Actually an alpaca.

80

82

84

87

Chapter Eight
A Major Probllama

This castle is so . . . BIG!

And SO . . . CASTLEY! SO . . . FULL OF QUOKKAS!

But if I want to get my butt on that throne, I need to be brave and get rid of that concrete-loving, quokka-obsessed evil llama, Sir Spits-A-Lot!

91

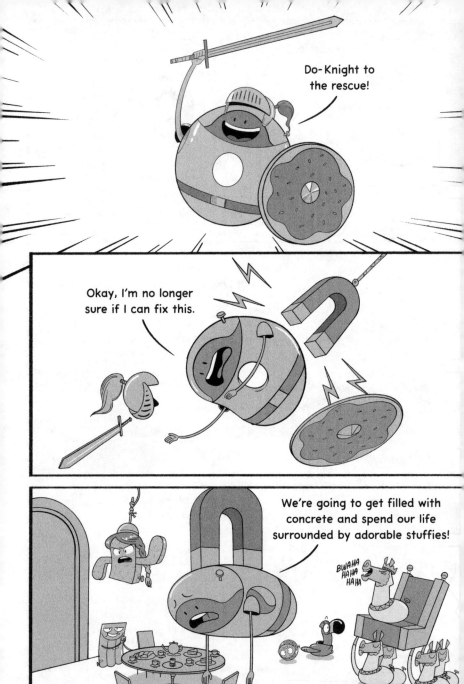

Chapter Nine

Not-So-Musical Statues

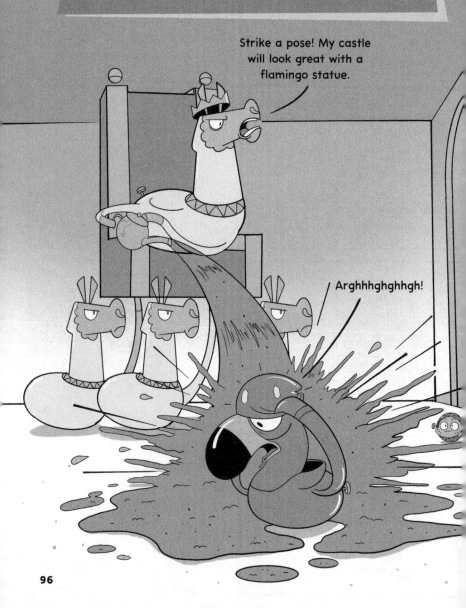

97

And how about a joke before you get turned into a statue? Which nunya is the nozzle I'm going to use to fill you with concrete? Nunya business! Mwahahahahaha!

This is what you get for trying to take my castle away!

You won't be needing this when you're made of stone!

BELIEVE IN YOURSELF
- CLOAK -
MEDIUM

You're right! If I'm going to be turned into a statue for air-ternity, at least let me look gla-mingo. Lynn, toss me that mirror!

99

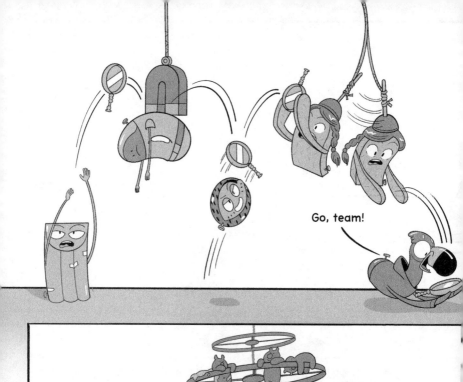

Go, team!

No one turns my friends into statues without a fight!

This CANNOT be happening! Those piñata wannabes can't hear me over choir practice!

Llama Mia! Here we blow again. Lla-ma, how can I resist you?

So I did defeat you after all?

103

104

Chapter Ten
His Royal Butt Cheeks

Um, Flamingo, you look kind of . . . uncomfortable?!

THE THRONE HURTS MY BUTT! Let's go on a castle tour instead!!

But before we do . . . I just wanted to say I'm so happy you guys FINALLY get a home that is as special, glamorous, fancy, and brilliant as you—my inflata-besties for life.

Awww!

Now, let's go see all the rooms!

LYNN'S GLAM PAD
A nail bar for Lynn

THE ROCK

DONUT'S SNACKS AND GIGGLES
A snacking and joke-writing room

FLAMINGO'S FANCY FITTING ROOM
All Flamingo's best outfits

So, um, all these rooms are nice . . . or at least nice-*ish*. And I bet the pool's amazing.

ROOM OF SPARKLES

This is fun? Right? And what's this? A crystal beach ball?

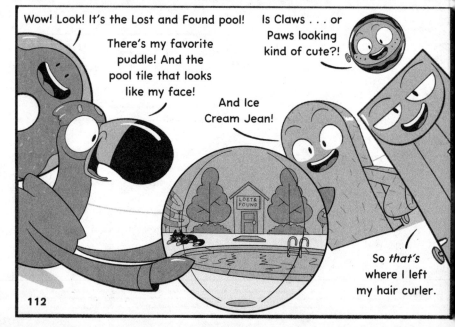

Wow! Look! It's the Lost and Found pool!

There's my favorite puddle! And the pool tile that looks like my face!

Is Claws . . . or Paws looking kind of cute?!

And Ice Cream Jean!

LOST & FOUND

So *that's* where I left my hair curler.

114

There's No Pllace Llike Home

There!

LOST & FOUND
PALACE

Home sweet home at last! I missed you, snacks! I missed you, pajamas!

This really is inflata-heaven on inflata-earth.

121

READY TO MAKE SOME MORE WAVES?

TURN THE PAGE TO SEE ALL THE INFLATA-FUN!

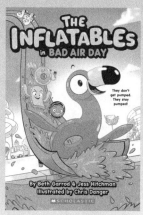

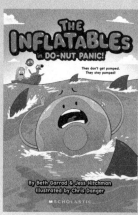
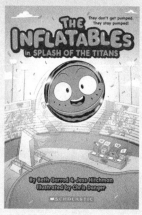
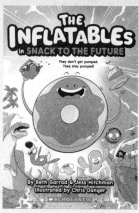